The Birders

An Unexpected Encounter
in the Northwest Woods

ROB ALBANESE

little bigfoot
an imprint of sasquatch books
seattle, wa

Every day was the same for Mr. Flynn, who wondered
if all his adventures were behind him . . .

until he saw a flash of white feathers.

Across the street, the days were boring for Ollie McPhee,
who thought nothing interesting ever happened . . .

until his mom said he could go outside.

I already did a long time ago. Here. You can draw it while I go look for the owl.

Oh, no. My memory works fine. I'm going to see that owl I already saw. REMEMBER?
WAIT! I'm coming too!

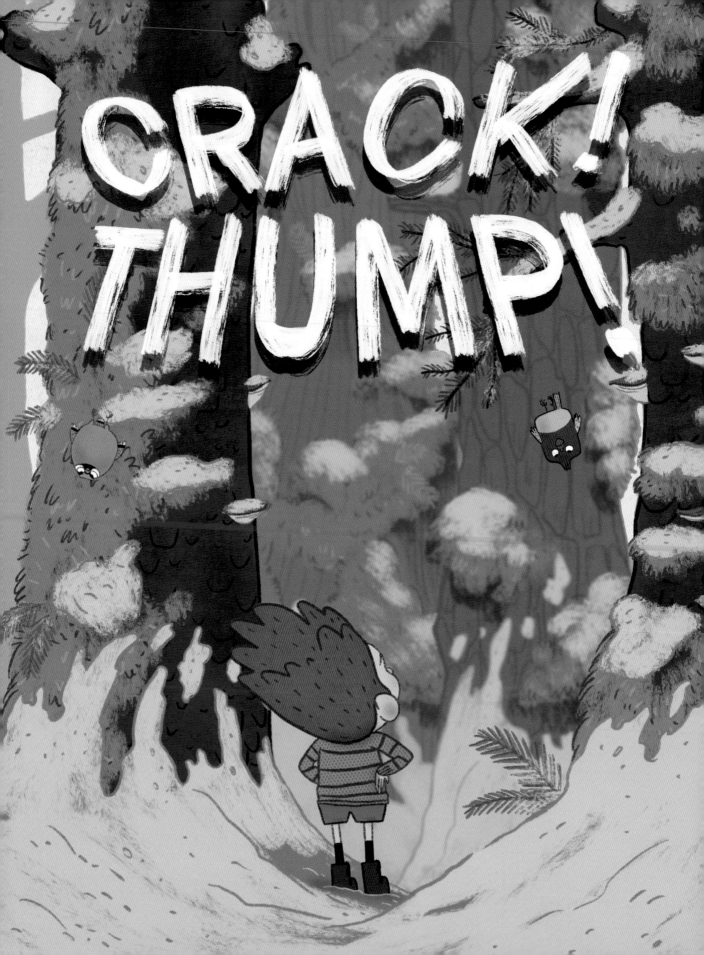

Oh, flappity finch!!!
I don't think you're supposed to say that.
I'm stuck, Ollie. Go get help.

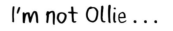

You might scare it when you get down. Your knees sound like popcorn when you move.
Well, I guess you could take a picture.

click click

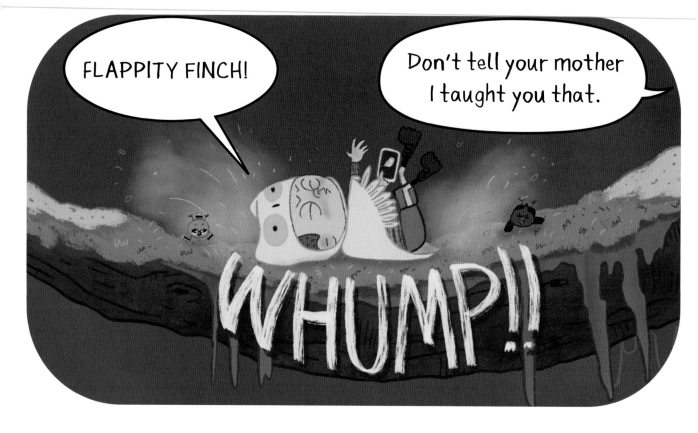

The next day, Ollie McPhee sat by his window, bored again . . .

until his mom said he could go outside.

Across the street, Mr. Flynn was flipping through his birding journal when he looked out the window and had an idea.

Don't worry, Mr. Flynn, I'm not gonna trip you today.

Our adventure yesterday reminded me of why I keep a birding journal—

How to Keep a Birding Journal

1. Find a notebook or gather together some paper.

2. Get something to write with.

3. Get ready and go outside.

4. Look for birds— where they are and what they are doing.

5. Record your observations.

6. Share your passion with someone else.

Where Do Snowy Owls Live?

Snowy owls live in the arctic *tundra* (a flat, treeless region) where their main source of food is lemmings. During winter, some snowy owls regularly migrate as far south as the northern continental United States.

However, during an *irruptive year* (a sudden increase in population), the snowy owls can migrate as far south as Florida. Snowy owl irruptions are usually associated with an increase in the lemming population.

When away from the tundra, snowy owls can usually be found in similar habitats. They like to perch on fences, buildings, and sometimes trees, where they can survey large wide-open spaces like fields and even airports. If you are lucky enough to see a snowy owl, please observe it from a distance so as not to disturb its natural behavior.

To H and E,
you inspire all
my stories

Manufactured in China by Printplus Ltd. in July 2021

LITTLE BIGFOOT with colophon is a registered
trademark of Penguin Random House LLC

26 25 24 23 22   9 8 7 6 5 4 3 2 1

Editor: Daniel Germain
Production editor: Bridget Sweet
Designer: Anna Goldstein

Library of Congress Cataloging-in-Publication Data
Names: Albanese, Rob, author, illustrator.
Title: The birders : an unexpected encounter in the northwest woods /
Rob Albanese.
Description: Seattle, WA : Little Bigfoot, an imprint of Sasquatch Books,
   [2022] | Audience: Ages 5-9. | Audience: Grades 2-3. |
Identifiers: LCCN 2021024196 | ISBN 9781632173638 (hardcover)
Subjects: CYAC: Graphic novels. | Bird watching--Fiction. | Old
   age--Fiction. | Friendship--Fiction. | LCGFT: Graphic novels. |
Picture books.
Classification: LCC PZ7.7.A347 Bi 2022 | DDC 741.5/973--dc23
LC record available at https://lccn.loc.gov/2021024196

ISBN: 978-1-63217-363-8

Sasquatch Books
1904 Third Avenue, Suite 710
Seattle, WA 98101

SasquatchBooks.com

FSC
www.fsc.org

MIX
Paper from
responsible sources
FSC® C001701

ROB ALBANESE always knew he wanted to be an artist and storyteller; it just took him a long time to get there. Rob loves all aspects of the natural world. He can often be found hiking with his family through a forest or searching a beach at low tide for spectacular creatures. Birding is a new way he has found to connect with nature.

Visit him at RobSketches.com.

Ollie's Bird Journal

Snowy Owl

Osprey

· with mr. Flynn

Bald eagle
· white head

· fish
· water